SCARECROW MAGIC

For Barb. Thank you for many years of loving support. Hopefully, this will
help you overcome your fear of corn mazes. –E.M.

For Aaron, who made Halloween hideous and hilarious. –M.M.

Text copyright © 2015 by Ed Masessa
Illustrations copyright © 2015 by Matt Myers
All rights reserved. Published by Orchard Books, an imprint of Scholastic Inc., *Publishers since 1920*. ORCHARD BOOKS and design are registered trademarks of Watts Publishing Group, Ltd., used under license. SCHOLASTIC and associated logos are trademarks and/or registered trademarks of Scholastic Inc. • No part of this publication may be reproduced, stored in a retrieval system, or transmitted in any form or by any means, electronic, mechanical, photocopying, recording or otherwise, without written permission of the publisher. For information regarding permission, write to Scholastic Inc., Attention: Permissions Department, 557 Broadway, New York, NY 10012.

Library of Congress Cataloging-in-Publication Data
Masessa, Ed, author.
Scarecrow magic / by Ed Masessa ; drawn by Matt Myers. — First edition.   pages   cm
Summary: When night falls and the moon appears, magic is in the air and Scarecrow comes alive and plays with all his ghoulish and ghostly friends.
ISBN 978-0-545-69109-3
1. Scarecrows—Juvenile fiction. 2. Magic—Juvenile fiction. 3. Stories in rhyme. [1. Stories in rhyme. 2. Scarecrows—Fiction. 3. Magic—Fiction.] I. Myers, Matt, illustrator. II. Title.   PZ8.3.M41947Sc 2015   [E]—dc23   2014030746

10 9 8 7 6 5 4 3 2 1   15 16 17 18 19
Printed in Malaysia   108   First printing, July 2015

The text type was set in Avenir 85 Heavy. The display type was set in Coop Flaired. Book design by Chelsea C. Donaldson

SCARECR

by **Ed Masessa** • illustrated by **Matt Myers**

DW MAGIC

rchard Books · New York · An Imprint of Scholastic Inc.

Glow from the moon, so full and so bright,

A cool autumn breeze turns the air crisp and light.

Hung from a post, a man made of straw

Moves a finger, a hand, an eyebrow, a jaw.

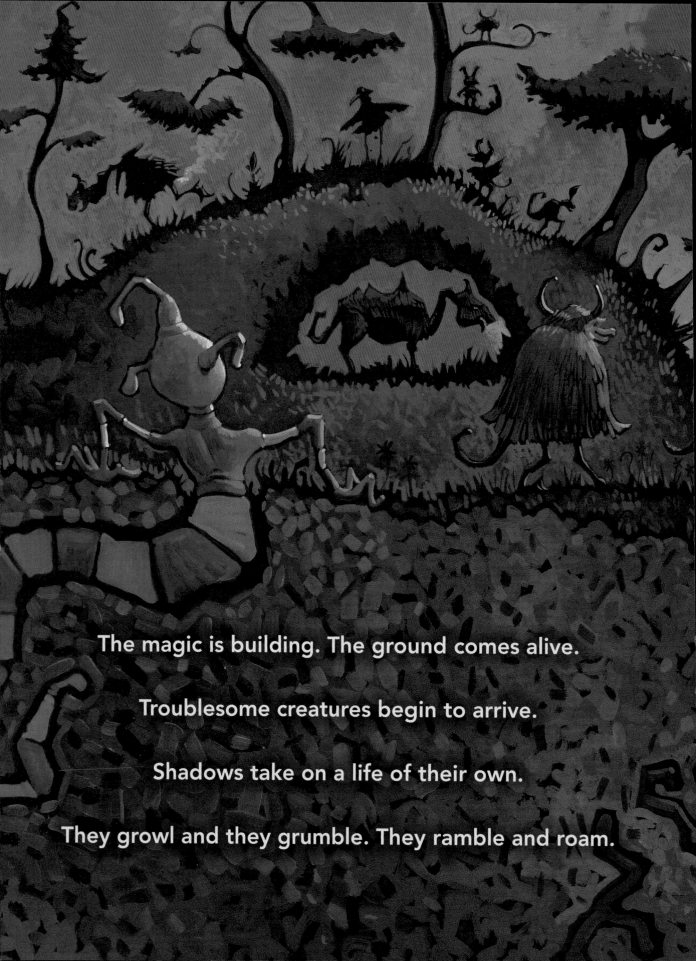

The magic is building. The ground comes alive.

Troublesome creatures begin to arrive.

Shadows take on a life of their own.

They growl and they grumble. They ramble and roam.

Some are bald as a pumpkin, some covered with hair.

Excitement is growing in the chilly night air.

The man made of straw knows the time is just right.

He loosens the ropes that are binding him tight.

He jumps from his post, landing light as a pin.

With a zip and a swoosh, he slips out of his skin.

Bones rattle and sway in their own clever way.

His day job is done, and he's ready to play.

He creaks and he croaks as he belts out a tune.

Ghoulies and ghosties dance under the moon.

Goblins jump rope with a double-Dutch vine.

Bones boy hops in, stepping in time.

Long, lumpy gourds stand pinned to the ground.

Round, knobby pumpkins roll them all down.

From under the leaves, a pair of eyes peeks.

Critters all hide while skeleton seeks!

Stones become marbles. Rocks become jacks.

Ghosties appear, bringing slugballs for snacks.

Slimy fresh worms—a delectable treat!

A ghoul's favorite snack has the odor of feet.

Crusty cornstalks make good swords to wage battle.

Scarecrow joins in—you can hear his bones rattle.

Soon playtime is over. The sun starts to rise.

Goblins and ghoulies must all say good-bye.

Some blend into shadows. Some burrow down low.

Some tidy the field so no one will know.

Back on his post, Scarecrow zips up his skin.

Fun time has ended. Soon work must begin.

With a wink and a nod, he bids them good night—

His ghoulish young friends, all hidden from sight.

But he knows that the magic will return one night soon,

On a chilly clear night, in the light of the moon.